THE

WANIGAN

A LIFE ON THE RIVER

ALSO BY GLORIA WHELAN

Goodbye, Vietnam

Hannah

Next Spring an Oriole

Night of the Full Moon

Shadow of the Wolf

Silver

Mrs. Gaunt

Whelan, Gloria.

The wanigan.

THE WANIGAN
A LIFE ON THE RIVER

BY

GLORIA WHELAN

ILLUSTRATED BY

EMILY MARTINDALE

ALFRED A. KNOPF
NEW YORK

THIS IS A BORZOI BOOK PUBLISHED BY ALFRED A. KNOPF

Published in the United States of America by Alfred A. Knopf, a division of Random House, Inc., New York, and simultaneously in Canada by Random House of Canada Limited, Toronto. Distributed by Random House, Inc., New York.

The following poems by Edgar Allan Poe are excerpted in the text:
"Tamerlane" (1827), "Al Aaraaf" (1829), "Alone" (1830), "The City in the Sea" (1831), "To Helen" (1831), "The Sleeper" (1831), "To One in Paradise" (1834), "Dreamland" (1844), "The Raven" (1845), "Ulalume" (1847).

www.randomhouse.com/kids

Library of Congress Cataloging-in-Publication Data

Whelan, Gloria.
The wanigan : a life on the river / by Gloria Whelan.
p. cm.
Summary: In 1878, eleven-year-old Annabel and her parents survive a year of adventure that includes floating downriver in two shacks along with a group of Michigan lumbermen moving logs.
ISBN 0-375-81429-9 (trade) — ISBN 0-375-91429-3 (lib. bdg.)
[1. Logging—Fiction. 2. Lumbermen—Fiction. 3. Frontier and pioneer life—Michigan—Fiction. 4. Michigan—Fiction.] I. Martindale, Emily, ill. II. Title.

PZ7.W5718 Wan 2002
[Fic]—dc21 2001038097

Printed in the United States of America
April 2002
10 9 8 7 6 5 4 3 2 1

First Edition

For Alyse,
whose great-great-grandfather
was a lumberjack

CONTENTS

ON THIS HOME BY HORROR HAUNTED

I will be forced to live in low circumstances. The crude shack in which I will dwell will have no resting place but will move continually. I will not be where I was the day before or where I'll be the next day. All around me will be nothing but the river, the logs, and the wanigan.

I don't blame Mama and Papa. They are victims of tragic circumstances. Three years ago, in the year of our Lord 1875, when I was but eight years old, Papa bought a farm in the northern part of Michigan. Until then we had lived in Detroit, where Papa had worked as a wheelwright, making wheels for wagons and barrows.

When he and Mama heard of land for sale, they spread out a map of Michigan. They showed me how all of northern Michigan was a lovely green color.

"Green to grow things on," Papa said. "The gentleman who wants to sell the farm tells of land that is hungry for a plow. He says a man can own more acres than he could walk over in a day. He promises wild berries in the meadows, game in the forests, and fish in the rivers, all there for the taking. The price of land is cheap," Papa said. "Why shouldn't we have our bit of it?"

We had a selling-up of our house in Detroit. Someone walked through it, poking into the cupboards and corners, owning it before they bought it. The auctioneer came and sang all our furniture away. People carried off Mama's rocker and my bed. They took away the china, thin as eggshell, that Grandma had left us. It was like a merciless wind blowing through our home. "Papa," I wailed, "they're stealing everything." Papa had to explain to me what was happening.

I was relieved to see Mama hang on to our best dresses and keep back her books and Grandma's tea set from the auction. I imagined that on our new land I would sit beside a stream and would read my favorite poems.

Mama says that like her, I have a delicate and tender nature. Every day I improve my mind by learning some lines from one of the great poets in Mama's book of poems. My favorite poet is Mr. Edgar Allan Poe. My name is Annabel Lee, just like the name of one of Mr. Poe's poems. Mr. Poe wrote these words:

From childhood's hour I have not been
As others were—I have not seen
As others saw.

I think that is very lovely. His words are true of me for I am always watching out for things of beauty. Unhappily, where we are now, there are few things of beauty.

We left Detroit with high hopes. Papa had the look on him of someone who has opened a book he can't wait to be reading. He said we'd grow potatoes big as pumpkins and pumpkins too big to get your arms around. Mama was all plans. She had a bolt of cloth for curtains and chair covers. She said our rooms would be filled with wildflowers from the woods.

With many kisses and promises of writing to one another, I said farewell to my best friend, Mary. The only thing that kept me from shedding tears was my dream of our new home, with me picking roses from our garden and gathering apples from our orchard.

I sat in the wagon holding on to my small dog. I called him Bandit because the black fur around his eyes made him look like he was wearing a mask. I told him soon he would be running through the woods making friends with all the wild animals.

Papa was badly cheated. Our house was only a cabin. The snow crept through the chinking as if it meant to bury us. There wasn't a soul around for miles to admire Mama's curtains. The land was all sand. It grew nothing but rocks. Our crops wilted and our cow died.

On the worst day of all, Bandit was out in the yard gnawing on a venison bone. The bone was left over from a deer Papa had shot to keep food on the table. We heard a terrible howl like a scream. Then more snarling howls. Papa ran outside. Mama hung on to me and wouldn't let me go after Papa. Bandit had gotten into a fight with a coyote.

The winter ground was too hard to bury Bandit, so Papa made a wooden box. Mama lined it with warm flannel. When spring came and the ground softened, we buried Bandit and I planted daisies on his grave.

That summer the well where we got our water dried up. Every ear of corn we shucked was ugly and useless with corn borers. At last we gave up. Papa got a poor price for our farm. To put bread in our mouths, he took a job as a lumberjack. Mama, though unused to such hard work, assisted the camp cook.

It was a sad two days' journey from the farm to the lumber camp. The camp was very rough. The men were loud and coarse. Papa, Mama, and I had a little room, which Mama made as tidy and comfortable as she could. Papa made a shelf for her books and Mama set out Grandma's tea set. Unfortunately, our room was next to the kitchen, so some days it smelled like sauerkraut and some days it smelled like dried codfish.

In the bunk rooms the men slept upon straw, which they called marsh feathers. They chewed tobacco and did not care where they spit. They slept in their clothes with their heads resting on "turkeys," sackcloth bags that held their extra clothes. Nothing got washed until Sunday, which was called, most inelegantly, boil-up day. The rest of the time their dirty, wet socks were draped over the rafters of the bunk room to dry.

In spite of their coarseness, Mama was friendly to all the men. If they forgot their manners and spit in her presence, she pulled in her skirts and looked the other way.

Mama was never too tired to school me. When she was only eighteen, her parents had died of typhoid fever and she had been left to make her own way in the world. She became a teacher. Numbers and spelling were old friends to her. Together we did sums and read from Mama's books of poems. Though Mama encouraged me to turn to more cheerful poems, I always chose Mr. Poe because his poems were so melancholy. I was sure he could have turned our unhappy experiences into a lovely, sad poem that would bring tears to the eyes of all who read it.

Each afternoon Mama set the kettle to boil, put a spoonful of tea leaves into Grandma's teapot, and poured us a cup of tea. While we drank from the dainty cups, Mama told me stories of the house she had lived in as a girl. It had a big front porch with a swing. "And a lawn, Annabel, with beautiful green grass."

As she spoke, I looked around the camp. Since there was little there of beauty, Mama's stories and Mr. Poe's poems were a great comfort. Still, I was sure I was not meant to waste away in such unrefined company and in so uncivilized a place.

I did all that I could to raise myself above my sad surroundings. I kept my clothes neat, and I tied up my hair each night in rags so that it curled in a pretty way. I shined my boots, and before I went to bed I rubbed a bit of lard into my hands to keep them soft. Nothing I did could rid my hair or my clothes of the odor of the pine trees. The smell of pine was everywhere. We breathed it and ate it and slept with it.

I drew up a calendar and counted off the days until the winter would be over. I kept myself apart from the men and had nothing whatsoever to do with the chore boy, Jimmy.

It appeared to me that the only purpose in life for the men was to see how many trees they could cut down. All day long I heard the cry "Timber" as the giant pine trees fell. The choppers cut nicks in the trees. The sawyers cut the trees down. The swampers lopped off the branches. The sprinkling wagons laid down a layer of water, which turned to ice in the freezing Michigan winter. The skidders slid the logs over the ice to the sleighs. The loaders put them on the sleighs, and the teamsters hitched up the ox team and pulled the sleighs over the ice to the river. There along the riverbank the logs were stacked into great wooden walls awaiting spring.

At last the snow melted, the spring rains came, and the river rose. In winter the river had minded its own business. Now, suddenly, it was flooding onto the banks.

With much excitement the men placed a charge of dynamite amongst the logs. There was a terrible boom and a great roar. I put my hands over my ears and hid under the bed. The men shouted and cheered. The logs came crashing down into the water to begin their float down the Au Sable River to Oscoda and Lake Huron and the sawmills at the river's mouth. The journey through miles of wilderness would take three months.

I was glad to see those logs go. I hoped that now that it was spring, we would return to Detroit and civilization. With a sigh Mama explained that we didn't have enough money. I had to bite my lip to keep from crying.

"Papa and four other men will follow the logs as they float down the river," Mama said. "You should be proud of your father, Annabel. Only the best of the loggers are chosen. Their job will be to rescue any logs belonging to our company that are hung up on the shore. At night your papa and the other men will sleep on a floating bunkhouse that will trail down the river behind the wanigan."

"The wanigan, Mama?"

"The wanigan is a little floating house where I will do the cooking and where you and I will sleep for the three months it will take the logs to make their way down the river."

I imagined the wanigan would be something like our dear little white house in Detroit, with its small sitting room and my little bedroom. I even hoped there would be a porch with chairs where Mama and Papa and I could sit and watch the river. It was not to be.

Imagine my disappointment as I stood shivering at the river's edge watching the camp's carpenters fling rough, worn boards every which way to build two ugly shacks upon two ugly scows.

"But, Mama," I said, "the carpenters must have made a mistake. There is only one room in the wanigan."

"It will be a kitchen by day, Annabel, and a bedroom for us by night."

When Mama saw my disappointment, she tried to cheer me. "Think how cozy you and I will be with the kitchen's stove to warm us."

"Mama, you said we would be on the wanigan three months. What about the hot stove in July?"

"The river will cool us, Annabel." Mama sighed. "We must make the best of things. With the money Papa and I make this summer, we will be able to buy a small house in Detroit."

With that hope I had to be satisfied.

When I had my first look inside the wanigan, my heart sank. The two narrow cots that Mama

and I would sleep on would be put down at night and taken up in the morning, so that during the day there would be no bit of the wanigan that was all mine. There would be no room for Papa, who would sleep with the other men. It would be the first time I had been separated from Papa, and I thought it would be lonely on the wanigan without him.

We would live for months in this shack, moving by day and tied up to shore at night. I imagined bears and wolves climbing into the wanigan while we slept. The most humiliating thing of all: I heard the chore boy, Jimmy, call Papa and the other men who would float down the river with us by the hateful name of river pigs.

Such, for the next months, will be my miserable life. As Mr. Poe says, "*On this home by Horror haunted . . .*"

LONE WATERS, LONE AND DEAD

The evening of the first day of May, Mama and I boarded the wanigan. There were bits of ice like frozen lace along the edges of the river. Tatters of snow lay deep in the woods. I was still wearing my scratchy long underwear.

Though the stove gave off some warmth, I shivered in my bed. I heard the sound of the coyotes howling. I thought of Bandit and put my hands over my ears.

It was my habit each night to escape my

unhappy fate by imagining myself in some faraway time or country. This night I pretended I was riding a camel across the desert on my way to an Arabian palace. The sun shone and I swayed gracefully on top of the camel. At last I fell asleep to the kitchen smells of cinnamon and dried apples.

Sometime before dawn I heard Mama getting dressed. Through the cracks in the wanigan the river mumbled and grumbled to itself. I turned over and settled into the warm spot I had made in the bed.

I lay there thinking that as crude as the cabin in the woods had been and as coarse as the lumber camp was, the wanigan was worse. Every day I would have to get used to a new place I had never seen before and would never see again. I said to myself that I was the most unhappy person in the world. Feeling very sorry for myself, I folded my cot and put my quilts away. I splashed water on my face, slipped into my dress, and pulled on my wool stockings. When I looked out the wanigan's one window, there was nothing but the dark looking back at me.

Mama was busy preparing breakfast for the men. The kitchen was full of shifting shadows from the kerosene lamp that swung from the rafters, calling to mind Mr. Poe's

> *. . . o'er the floor and down the wall,*
> *Like ghosts the shadows rise and fall!*

There was a pot of coffee boiling on the cookstove and a pot of oatmeal so thick I could hardly stir it. Bacon was sizzling in the pan, and the griddle was covered with morning glories. That's what the men called Mama's buckwheat pancakes. Mama sent me out on deck to bang two frying pans together to summon the men from the bunk shack.

I watched the men and the chore boy, eager for their breakfast, jump from the bunk shack to the wanigan. They hurried past me to crowd into the cook shack. The sand and mud from their boots dirtied the floor. There was no room for a table and chairs in the wanigan, so Papa and the other men, along with the chore boy, ate where they could. They heaped the food onto their tin plates and poured coffee into their pannikins. The pannikins, tin cups with no handles, warmed the men's cold hands.

There was much reaching and grabbing. "Give me the tin cow," one of the men said, snatching a can of milk right out of Papa's hand. Another man grabbed a pitcher and poured a flood of molasses onto his pancakes.

The chore boy reached for the margarine. "Hand me the axle grease," he said.

Only Papa, with his quiet voice and neatly combed hair, looked to be a gentleman. The other men, with their loud voices and untidy clothes, did not.

Penti Ranta, stocky and red-faced, is a Finn who fought in the war to preserve the Union. Thomas Johnson, whom the men call Big Tom, is an Indian. I don't believe I have heard above five words from him. Frenchy de Rossier, with his bushy beard and the wide red sash he always wears around his waist, looks like a pirate. He comes from Canada and speaks in a crude jumble of English and

French. Teddy McGuire is Irish. Unhappily, his son, Jimmy, accompanies him. Jimmy is the chore boy and a terrible trial to me. He is clumsy and careless and leaves behind him a trail of broken crockery. Nothing gives Jimmy greater pleasure than to mock my manners and breeding by calling me Princess Annie. Such are my companions on this May morning.

I must admit that all the men are respectful of Mama. With her neatly braided black hair, her long, tapered fingers, and her graceful and elegant ways, they can see that she was gently brought up. Although they call her Gussie when her name is Augusta, they are quick to lift a heavy pot or move a barrel of flour for her. They always have a kind word for her cooking. They try not to curse or spit in the wanigan. Not spitting is hard for them. Their cheeks, like those of a squirrel gathering acorns, grow so fat with tobacco juice I am afraid they will burst.

On this first morning Frenchy was quick to compliment Mama on the coffee. "Dat's strong enough to grow de *cheveux*, de hair, on de turnip, ma'am," he said.

With no niceties observed, breakfast was over in mere moments. The men took out their oilcloth lunch bags. They stuffed the bags with bacon, biscuits, hard cheese, oatmeal cookies, and dried prunes, which they call logging berries.

Then came the disgusting part. The men rolled up their trousers, which they shorten to keep out of the way of their spiked boots. They removed their socks and shoes. Scooping up handfuls of lard, the men rubbed the lard onto their feet. Next came three pair of socks and heavy boots greased with beeswax and tallow. The men would be in and out of the freezing water pushing the stranded logs off the shore and into the river. I knew their feet must be kept dry. Thank heavens they obeyed Mama and took the lard from a special bucket she had set aside for just that use.

I watched the men walk the wanigan, with Mama and me right in it, down the river to its new docking. A man on either side had stuck sharp pike poles into the riverbed. Hanging on to the pikes, the men walked from the front of the wanigan to the rear, pushing the cooking shack and the bunk shack that was tied to it as they went. In between the walks, the men let the swift current push the wanigan even farther down the river. When the men had made many such walks back and forth and the wanigan was just where they wanted it, they brought it close to shore. They dropped anchor and climbed over the side to begin their work, leaving us to discover where we would spend this day. Next day the wanigan would be moved again. In this way we would travel the hundred and seventy miles to Oscoda.

Papa was the last to leave. He gave me a quick hug and waded ashore. Mama watched, too. She stood beside me, a worried look on her face. She always hated to say goodbye to Papa in the mornings. In the winter there had been the danger of Papa being crushed under falling trees. On this trip there were new dangers. I had overheard the men say that on the river drive there were sure to be slippery logs, deep water, and dangerous logjams.

I stood on the deck watching Papa disappear into the woods. Like Mama, I worried that something might happen to him. I feared my dear papa might meet some tragic fate in Mr. Poe's *"lone waters, lone and dead . . . still waters, still and chilly."*

The early-morning light was thin as skim milk. Overhead a V of geese headed north. The geese sounded like Gabriel's horn, the long tin horn that had called the men to meals back in the lumber camp.

On one side of the river there was nothing along the shore but empty fields and a crop of tree stumps left behind by the loggers. On our side of the river, where there had been no logging, the pine trees soared more than a hundred feet. Even if I stretched my neck, I could not see to the trees' tops. Ahead of the wanigan floated thousands of logs, so that the whole river looked like it was made of wood.

My unhappy thoughts at what lay before me were interrupted by a terrible crashing and banging of pans from inside the wanigan. Jimmy collected wood for the stove and polished the stove with blacking to keep it from rusting. It was also one of his jobs to scrub the pots. It was a job Jimmy detested. I had heard him say to his father, "Why must I stay with the women? I can free up the logs along the shore as well as any man."

Teddy McGuire shook his head. "You're only twelve, son. That's no job for a boy. One misstep in that raging river and you're done for. Don't whine, there's a good boy. I don't need to have the likes of you causing me grief. I've enough to worry me."

Mama went into the kitchen to see to all the commotion. I stayed out on the deck of the wanigan to avoid being in the same room with Jimmy, who was sure to find some way to torment me.

Just as I feared, I soon found Jimmy beside me. Once the pots were cleaned, Mama was glad to get him out of the kitchen. Jimmy is tall for his age and skinny, with large, clumsy hands and ragged nails because he bites them. His feet are large, too, so that he looks like a puppy with big paws who will grow into a great dog. He has red hair, which his father calls ginger. His father cuts Jimmy's hair and one side never matches the other. Jimmy has no mother to care for him, so that his shirts were missing many buttons until Mama sewed them on for him.

Jimmy's story is a truly tragic one. His mother died a year ago. Papa said it was diphtheria and Jimmy had it as well. After his wife's death Teddy McGuire was left to care for Jimmy. Since lumberjacking was all Teddy McGuire knew, he took his son along with him. Jimmy became the chore boy in camp. I pity Jimmy having no mother to care for him.

Once I expressed my deep sorrow at the death of his mother, but Jimmy said it was none of my business and ran away. Mama said it was too hard for him to talk about his mother's death. Even so, I thought he needn't have been so churlish.

That morning I had no wish to speak with Jimmy and pretended to be studying the shore.

Jimmy stared most impolitely at my feet. "If you had a proper pair of boots," he said, "instead of those fancy laced kid-leather things that aren't good for anything, you could go along the bank with me. You could help me pick up firewood for the kitchen stove."

It was my dearest wish that Jimmy would just disappear. "I haven't the least desire to accompany you anywhere."

"You're so stuck-up, Princess Annie, it's a wonder you can bear to breathe the same air everyone else does."

While it's true I pride myself on my manners and deplore those of the lumberjacks, no one wishes to be called stuck-up, especially when they aren't at all. I felt my lip trembling and tears start up. I did not see how I could spend weeks and weeks shut into a tiny cabin with no company but a cruel boy.

I turned my face away but not quickly enough.

"Hey," he said, "you don't have to blubber. If you can't stand for me to be on the wanigan with you, I'll get my own barge."

Jimmy swung himself from the wanigan onto a huge pine log floating in the river. He stretched out on his back as if the log were a couch and waved to me. The log floated along with hundreds of other logs on the river's flood. A moment later it bumped into another log, and Jimmy was flailing about in the icy water. He climbed out of the river, leaking water from his cap to his boots. As he jumped onto the bunk shack to change his clothes, he gave me a furious look. I kept my countenance, but it was hard not to smile.

THIS HAUNTED WOODLAND

Mama called me inside the wanigan. The whole shack had the sour, yeasty smell of rising bread. Mama was looking tired, as she always does after the hard kneading of a big batch of dough.

"Annabel, I heard you talking with Jimmy. You are very hard on him. You ought to have a little consideration for the poor boy, motherless as he is."

I hated scoldings from Mama. She always

looked so sorrowful about my bad behavior, as if it truly hurt her. "But he's so rude," I told her.

"He is a little clumsy in his ways, but I believe he only wants to make friends with you. He doesn't know how to go about it. You must meet him halfway. Now help me set the loaves."

Relieved the scolding was over, I scooped up a handful of the dough, patting and folding it in the way Mama had taught me. The dough felt like the softest down pillow. The fragrant brown loaves that came out of the oven seemed a miracle to me.

When we finished setting the loaves, I soaked the dried apples for pies, peeled a great pile of potatoes, and shed tears over a peck of onions. All the while I worked, I was engaged in the learning of Mr. Poe's poetry. This day I had chosen the lines:

Well I know, now, this dank tarn of Auber,
This ghoul-haunted woodland of Weir.

I didn't understand exactly what the words meant, but the dark woodland on the one side of the wanigan truly appeared mysterious.

Mama was taking a moment to rest in the wanigan's single chair. Her face was pale and I saw she had pinned up her long hair any which way. It hurt me to see her so worn out. "Mama," I asked, "don't you get awfully tired of all this cooking? Don't you wish you were in a beautiful garden reading poetry with flowers all around you and servants to bring you a cool drink and little cakes with pink frosting?"

Mama sighed. "Annabel, what's the use of wishing for something that will never happen? It just makes you unhappy."

I wasn't so sure. I had lots of daydreams. When I was unhappy with what was around me, I could close my eyes and go where I wanted to be.

When I looked up, I saw Jimmy all dried off and standing at the doorway with a canvas sack of firewood. I wondered how much he had heard. Some of it, surely, for he said in a low, grudging voice, "If it's flowers you want, the whole woods is full of them. I could show you, only you got those silly things on." He pointed to my boots.

Before I could come up with a response to put Jimmy in his place, Mama said, "Annabel has an old pair of rubber boots she could put on." She gave me a meaningful look and said, "I'm sure it's very kind of Jimmy to offer to show you the flowers. Only don't go too far."

I loathed the old rubber boots. They made me feel ugly. Anyhow, the last thing in the world I wanted was to go wandering around in some desolate woods with Jimmy McGuire, but the look from Mama made me remember her scolding. I pulled on the boots while Jimmy stood there grinning. Jimmy has a wide mouth, so there was a lot of grin.

The wanigan was anchored close to the shore. I held up my skirts and walked carefully through the shallow water so as not to get my hem wet. Jimmy splashed his way to shore, showering me with water. I was sure he did it on purpose and I bit my tongue to keep from saying so.

Downstream we could see the men wrestling the huge logs that had been caught up on the shore. They would send the logs back into the river. After they had worked their way a few miles downstream, they would hike back to the wanigan. The next day they would move the wanigan and start all over again. I searched among the men, recognizing Papa by the black cap Mama had knitted for him.

As we clambered over a great pine log that lay along the shore, I asked, "Why didn't they push *this* log into the river?"

Jimmy pointed to one end of the log. Cut into the log were two triangles. "That's not our mark," Jimmy said. "Every outfit's got its own brand. Since that's not our brand, the men leave it be."

I remembered seeing our lumberjacks using

a marking hammer to hammer a star onto the ends of the logs before piling them up on the riverbank.

"Lots of lumber companies send their logs down the river, so that the logs are all mixed up," Jimmy said. "When the logs get to the mouth of the river, they'll be sorted according to their marks." He was happy to show off knowing more about something than I did.

Jimmy headed into the dark woods as if he knew exactly where he was going. I followed nervously, worrying about what was behind each tree. At last we escaped the woods and came to an open field. The May sun was as warm as a shawl on my shoulders. We had left the river smell behind, and what I smelled now was grass and earth, something I had not smelled since we had left our poor farm.

There had been woods all around our farm, but I didn't often venture into them. Mama had warned me not to go too far, reciting the poem about the babes in the woods who had gotten lost and died and the little birds who came and covered them with leaves. After hearing that poem, I was afraid of all the darkness in the woods and how one path looked like any other. Even now, though Jimmy seemed to know where he was going, I worried that we would end up lost and buried under a pile of leaves.

Whenever I thought of the farm, I thought of Bandit. I hadn't wanted to give away my feelings, especially to Jimmy, but before I could stop myself I said, "I really miss my dog, Bandit."

"Where is he?" Jimmy wanted to know.

"He got killed by a coyote."

"That's awful sad," Jimmy said. I could see he meant it.

I thought of how Jimmy had lost his mother, and I felt bad about complaining about my dog. I wanted to tell Jimmy that, but I couldn't figure out how to do it without making him run away, like he always did when you said something kind to him. I didn't want to be left in the woods by myself.

"Here's the flowers," Jimmy said. "Thousands of 'em." He peered over his shoulder at me as if he dared me to disagree with him.

I couldn't. The flowers were everywhere. It looked as if someone had rolled out a pink-and-yellow carpet so thick your feet would sink into it right up to your ankles. There had been no flowers like that on our stony, sandy farm or in the small yards and along the muddy streets of Detroit. I recited Mr. Poe's

All wreathed with fairy fruits and flowers,
And all the flowers were mine.

I should have known better. Jimmy looked at me as if I had taken leave of my senses. "I don't know about that," he said. "And they're not *all yours*." He pointed to some pink flowers whose tiny throats had delicate red stripes. "Them's spring beauties," he said. "And them yellow ones is trout lilies." The tiny lilies hung like golden bells on their slender green stems. "My ma taught me the names of the flowers," he said.

Before I could stop myself, I said, "I'm sorry your mother died, Jimmy."

Sure enough, Jimmy began running and I had to hurry to keep him in sight. Over his shoulder he called, "We better get back. I got to straighten up the bunk shack before the men see it."

At suppertime that evening, as he climbed from the bunk shack to the wanigan, Mr. McGuire whispered to me, "I'm glad to see you and Jimmy are becoming friends, Annabel. I'd like to see my boy learn ladies' gentle ways, and he has no ma to teach him."

I was pleased that Mr. McGuire should call me a lady, but as to teaching Jimmy gentle ways, I didn't think that was possible.

After supper the men lingered in the wanigan. The early-spring evening stayed as light as afternoon. I showed Papa how neatly I had written my lessons, and Papa told me how he had seen a fox and her two cubs in the woods. I wished that Mama and Papa and I could be by ourselves. In the lumber camp I had been able to retire to our little room. Here there was no escaping the noisy lumbermen.

Teddy McGuire unwrapped his fiddle from the oiled cloth that kept out the river's dampness. He began to scrape away at a sad tune. Penti Ranta got out his mouth organ and played along. Papa, who is a fine tenor, sang "Home, Sweet Home" in such a melancholy voice Mama wiped away a tear. For once, the rest of the men were quiet.

Frenchy broke the silence by calling out, "Give us 'Old Dan Tucker.'" Soon all the men, even Big Tom Johnson, were harmonizing about Old Dan Tucker, who was too late to come to supper, combed his hair with a wagon wheel, and washed his face with a frying pan. Though the songs they sang did not have the elegant words of one of Mr. Poe's poems, I could not keep from tapping my toe and singing along:

I danced with a gal
with a hole in her stockin',
And her heel kept a-knockin'
and her toes kept a-rockin'.

The men began to dance, swinging one another about. Frenchy bowed to Mama, and Papa took me by the arm. Teddy McGuire sawed away on his violin, and the rest of us swirled about, bumping into one another in the narrow space of the deck.

While the singing and dancing was going

on, Jimmy had been somewhere in the woods. Now he clambered onto the wanigan. He was holding something in his hands. He thrust it at me. It was a small, furry ball with a stubby, striped tail. Its eyes were closed. I was so surprised I nearly dropped it.

"You can have it," Jimmy said. "It's a baby raccoon."

"Jimmy," Teddy McGuire said, "you haven't been robbing raccoon nests?"

"Gosh, no, Dad. It must've fallen out of a tree or something. There wasn't any mother raccoon nearby." He grinned at me. "You can call it Bandit."

It had a black mask on its face, just like my dog. I turned eagerly to Papa. "Can I keep it?"

"He's quiet enough now, Annabel, but those fellows are plenty mischievous when they get a little bigger. You'll have to ask your ma."

Mama sighed. "We'll try it, but one day it's going to have to go back to the wild." I think she would have said no but for Jimmy bringing up the Bandit part. She knew how much I missed my dog.

At last the men quieted and one by one climbed from the wanigan to the bunk shack. Papa went last. I kissed him good night. Mama was asleep in a minute, but I lay awake listening to the river and the forest sounds. An owl hooted and somewhere farther away, coyotes howled. I was glad the raccoon was safe with me. We were in the middle of nowhere, and not even yesterday's nowhere or tomorrow's. Though the Bible said envy was the rottenness of bones, still I envied children who lived in a real house that stayed where it was supposed to. I envied children who went to school in the morning and when they got home in the afternoon, there was their house, just where they left it.

I missed our city life in Detroit. I missed the dry-goods store, where Mama and I would admire the bolts of cloth. I missed the wide Detroit river, where Papa would point out the ships, telling me where they came from and what their names were.

To cheer me, I thought of how Jimmy had brought me the baby raccoon. I tiptoed to the box where Bandit was curled up on an old towel. Poor homeless critter, I thought, just like me. Then I remembered I had a mama and papa.

That day Mama and I had read from *The Tales of King Arthur and His Court*. I closed my eyes and imagined I was sitting by the side of Queen Guinevere in King Arthur's castle awaiting fair Sir Lancelot, to whom she had given her heart. In no time I was asleep.

IN THE MONTH OF JUNE

Though our surroundings changed each day, our rough life remained the same. The men searched out the logs that were hung up along the shore, Mama cooked, I helped, and in the evenings there were card games, rowdy songs, and often stories about the giant lumberjack Paul Bunyan.

Frenchy said, "Dat Paul Bunyan, he used de pine tree for de toothpick."

"When he got up in the morning," Big Tom

said, "Paul reached for a lake to use for his washbowl."

"And you know how he speeded up the logs?" Papa asked. "Paul Bunyan just straightened out the curves in the river."

"Why," said Penti Ranta, "that big man could clear a whole forest with one single swing of his ax."

Mama joined in. "It took hundreds of pigs to furnish his bacon and half a day to walk around one of his pancakes."

It was a rule that you could never repeat the Paul Bunyan story told by someone else but must make up your own. When it was my turn, I said, "Paul Bunyan kept a grizzly bear to scratch his back when it itched and to lie on his bed to keep his toes warm."

Jimmy said, "When Paul Bunyan wanted to

pay for something in a store, he just plunked a whole mountain right down on the counter and said to the storekeeper, 'There's gold in that mountain, but you got to get it out yourself.' "

I thought that was pretty good even if it was Jimmy who made it up.

Sundays were the men's only day of rest. One Sunday afternoon there was a birling contest. Penti Ranta and Big Tom climbed onto a floating log. Standing upright, the two men began rolling the log with their spiked boots. Faster and faster the log rolled while the men balanced themselves like tightrope walkers.

We all watched from the wanigan's deck. Papa bet Penti Ranta would be toppled first. Teddy McGuire and Frenchy bet it would be Big Tom. Penti Ranta was the first to splash into the river, leaving Big Tom standing. Papa

won two nickels and gave me one of them and Jimmy the other one.

Penti Ranta climbed on board soaking wet. It was nothing to him that the water was cold. Most mornings I had to stay in the wanigan and not look while Penti Ranta, naked as a jay, jumped into the river for his morning bath. He said everyone in Finland did that. When they came out of the cold water, they ran into a steam bath and got all sweaty again. He said every house had a steam bath called a sauna. Penti Ranta said we ought to make a sauna with the kitchen's woodstove. Mama said he'd have to put his clothes on before he came into her kitchen.

Most days when I was finished with my tasks and Jimmy had done his chores, we would explore the woods. While I still thought Jimmy unrefined, he was the only friend I had.

I even gave him my book of Mr. Poe's poetry to read, but the only poem he liked was "The Conqueror Worm," which was a horrible poem about dead people. "*'It writhes! It writhes!'*" Jimmy read in a voice so scary it made my blood creep. "*'A crawling shape,'*" he whispered in my ear.

When I tried to recite truly beautiful words of Mr. Poe's, like "*And the red winds are withering in the sky,*" Jimmy said, "That's dumb, Annie. I've never seen a red wind, and flowers wither, wind doesn't." At least now he just called me Annie instead of Princess Annie.

Papa had made Bandit a cage to keep him out of mischief. On our walks we took Bandit along to give him some exercise. We let him roll around in the grass and gave him tree-climbing practice.

At first I was reluctant to wander in such

wild country. I kept looking behind me, especially in the dark part of the woods, watching to be sure there were no coyotes around. Jimmy, who had grown up near a forest, bounded ahead, eager to show me his discoveries. Once it was a tree where a fat porcupine was settled on a high branch. On the ground beneath the tree was a pile of what happened after the porcupine ate. Only Jimmy would show someone something that disgusting.

Another time I ended up being sunk up to my knees in a bog. I recited Mr. Poe's lines:

By the grey woods, — by the swamp
Where the toad and the newt encamp . . .

Jimmy paid no attention but pointed to some strange plants with faces like tiny suns. I saw little hairs growing in a circle around the suns, and each hair had a drop of glistening dew. Nearby were plants shaped like a little pitcher.

"Your Mr. Poe would like those plants," Jimmy announced. "Those plants eat flies."

"I don't believe you," I said.

Sure enough, when he cut one open, there was a tiny fly.

"You don't know everything" was all I could think to say.

And he didn't, because the next day, even though I warned him not to, he took a stick to a hornets' nest that was hanging from a tree. When the hornets took off after us, we had to jump into the river to get away.

Another afternoon we found a little stream that ran into the river. A dam of sticks and mud was built across it, making a small pond.

"Beavers," Jimmy said.

We crawled up on the dam and began poking around. The dam was wonderfully fashioned. Though the sticks were helter-skelter, the beavers had glued them together with mud. Behind the dam the stream's river was backing up, making a lake and flooding the shore. Suddenly there was a terrible boom behind us. I jumped a mile. It was two beavers slapping their tails against the water. They were angry at our nosiness. Back and forth they swam, slapping their tails until we left.

It was already the middle of June. Every day there was something new to see. One day a yellow bird, another day a blue bird. The spring flowers were gone now, and in the dappled shade I gathered bouquets of field daisies and bouncing Bets for Mama.

I could see Mama was growing more and more tired. She could hide it from Papa because Papa slept in the bunk shack. He didn't see how gratefully she dropped onto her bed at night or how hard it was for her to get up in the dark mornings. When the weather was warm and the woodstove fired up, as it nearly always was, the wanigan was hot as Hades. Mama often had me dip cold water from the river into a bucket so that she could splash some over her face and hands. In the evenings she had always had a bit of mending or stitching in her hands, but now she sat quietly, watching the others, her hands idle in her lap.

One morning Mama suddenly collapsed onto the chair, too weak to get up. Her face was flushed and she was coughing. Frightened,

I started to call to Jimmy, who was on the shore, to run for Papa. Mama stopped me.

"Papa will only worry," she said. "And, Annabel, they might take my job as cook from me. If we are ever to have our own roof over our heads again, we need every penny." After a moment she took my hand in hers. Her hand was warm and dry, and I could feel the roughness from all her work. I recalled how when I was little, her hands were smooth and soft.

"You're quick at things, Annabel. You must cook the supper."

My heart sank. I hung on to her. "But, Mama, I don't know how."

"You've helped me all these weeks. You'll manage very well. I'll tell you what to do. First you must finish cutting up the meat." The day before the men had shot a deer and butchered it for the kitchen. "Tie my apron around you, dear, and watch how you handle that knife."

It turned my stomach to touch the grisly, bloody meat. When she put the meat on our plates, Mama would call it venison. Now it was all deer. Handling the raw meat, I remembered the shy and graceful animals Jimmy and I had seen so often in the woods. When the horrible work was finished, I put the pieces of meat along with potatoes, onions, and carrots into the big iron pot. Next I filled the pot with water and sprinkled in some salt and pepper and a couple of bay leaves that Mama kept in a jar. I was trying to roll out the crust for an apple pie when Jimmy climbed onto the wanigan and walked into the kitchen. I put my fingers to my lips and pointed to Mama, who was asleep on her cot.

The pie crust was sticking to the pastry board and my fingers. There was more dough on my hands than there was on the board. When I moved my hands, sticky strings of dough followed my fingers. I was ready to give up. Jimmy pointed to the flour barrel. I scooped up some flour and worked it into the dough. When it held together, I started rolling. Jimmy fitted the crust into the pan and filled it with apples. Because I knew he was trying to help, I kept quiet about his dirty hands, which had made the dough gray. In a half hour we had three pies in the oven. Unfortunately, I put them too close to the top. When they came out, the crust was burnt. Jimmy got a knife and scraped off the scorched part. I covered the tops with lots of sugar.

I swore Jimmy to secrecy and woke Mama just minutes before the men appeared. Only

Papa noticed something was wrong with Mama. The other men were busy with the stew, which was a little watery, and the pies, which were raggedy.

The spring flood was over and the river level was going down. More and more logs were stranded along the shore. As soon as dinner was over, the men pulled on their boots again and went off to work in the long, light evening.

Jimmy begged to go along and his father said he could. "Just this once. Only you're not to get in our way," Teddy McGuire warned.

Before they left, I saw Papa take Mama aside. Papa was saying something, but Mama was shaking her head. On his way out Papa gave me a hug. "I'm proud of you, Annabel," he whispered.

When we were alone, Mama said, "What would I have done without you today, Annabel?" She took my hand in hers and we watched the evening mists gather over the river. As the river disappeared among the white veils, it looked like we were anchored in the clouds.

"Mama," I asked, "will we ever have a proper home again, one that stays put?"

"I truly believe we will, Annabel. Your papa and I are saving all our wages from the lumber camp and the river drive. And there's the little we got from selling the farm. We want to go back to Detroit."

"And will we have our own house there?"

"Yes, Papa hopes to find a job on the river and a place to live along it."

"But not *in* the river?" I didn't want to

spend the rest of my life floating along like a log or a duck.

"No, Annabel. Papa means to build a little house, and you'll have a room of your own."

A room of my own, a place where I could open up a drawer and see my clothes all folded neatly. Perhaps Papa would build me a shelf for my books like he had built for Mama. Mama would hook a rug for the floor and make curtains. I'd help her make a quilt for my bed. And best of all, the room would have a door I could close. "Will I go to school?"

"There's sure to be a school nearby, Annabel. . . ."

Mama's voice trailed away. She was falling asleep. I stood alone for a moment on the deck of the wanigan. The moon was only a hazy shimmer through the mists. I thought of Mr. Poe's lines:

At midnight, in the month of June,
I stand beneath the mystic moon.

At last I went inside the wanigan. I couldn't help feeling a little proud that I had cooked supper and the supper had been eaten. I was so tired that for the first time ever I didn't bother turning up my hair in rag curlers. I closed my eyes and thought of Mama's promise that one day I would go to school. I smiled to myself, thinking that in a school I would be able to say poems and no one would laugh at me.

The next morning there was no lying in bed while Mama fixed breakfast. I hardly had time to splash water on my face before Mama was telling me how to mix the pancakes and grease the griddle. We had set the oatmeal to cook the night before, and now it was thick and bubbling. I had only to stir in some maple sugar. Mama managed to get the bacon in the oven and out of the oven when it was done. Jimmy, who had come with his morning load of firewood for the stove, helped me dump coffee grounds into the coffeepot. He filled the pot with water from the river and set it to boil.

"I watched my dad do it a hundred times," he said.

When the men came, they plunged into breakfast. Papa had a worried look on his face, but apart from Frenchy, the other men seemed not to notice how pale Mama was. Frenchy frowned as he watched Mama support herself by hanging on to the stove.

As the men packed their lunch, I was alarmed to see there would be no bread left for supper. I did not know how I was going to knead a big mess of dough, for I had seen how much trouble Mama had with it. I knew Mama couldn't do it.

When the other men were ready to leave, Frenchy called out, "I catch up wit you fellows. Got to nail de sole of my boot back on."

As soon as Papa and the other men were over the side, Frenchy took out the big wooden bread bowl, scooped up a pile of flour, and reached for the yeast jar, which Mama kept in the cooler, covered with a cloth. "My papa, he make de bread *chez nous*, at our house. He show me when I just a *petit garçon*, a little boy."

I winced as grains of tobacco from the pouch Frenchy carried around his neck kept falling into the bowl. In minutes the dough was mixed. Frenchy picked up the dough and slammed it over and over against the table, kneading and punching. "Dis dough be soft as a *bébé*'s bottom," he laughed. "Dis bread, it be *trés savoureux*, plenty tasty. But no fat loaves, Annabel." He stretched out his hands. "You make dem long and skinny like de tree branch." He patted me on the head. "We have de secret, *oui?*" The next minute he was gone.

Mama and I looked at one another. For a moment the weariness left her face and she smiled. "What a good man," she said.

What with the soaking of the beans and mixing them with molasses and ketchup and getting the fat pork back from Bandit, who had climbed up on the table and snatched it, and making enough frosting to fill the big crack that ran down the center of the cake I baked, the afternoon flew by. As I took the long, crusty loaves of bread from the oven, I felt sorry that I had once looked down my nose at Frenchy de Rossier and the way he talked.

MOUNTAINS TOPPLING EVERMORE

By the next week Mama was better. "You're not to worry, Annabel," she said. "It was only a touch of flu that settled in my chest. I'm much improved, thanks to your and Jimmy's help and the help of dear, sweet Frenchy."

I smiled as I thought of what Frenchy would think to hear himself called "dear, sweet Frenchy."

Mama got up from her bed in the morning and climbed into it at night with no deep sighs.

She was cross with Jimmy when he tracked mud into the kitchen and with me for leaning too close to the stove and scorching my apron, but she didn't have the strength for a severe scolding. Though Mama was cooking again, Jimmy and I still did a lot of the work. And each morning before he left, Frenchy started the bread.

With so much to do, there was no time to fret over my hard life. There was Mama to help, and Jimmy was forever dragging me off to show me something. Bandit was growing more and more mischievous each day. I could not even learn new lines of poetry but had to fall back on the ones I already knew.

It was the middle of July. Because the wanigan was so warm, I had taken to putting my cot out on the deck and sleeping outside. At first I was a little afraid of being right out in the open at night, but the moon was bright. Even on cloudy nights there were the small lights of fireflies among the grasses on the shore. One night I awoke to see veils of color sliding across the sky. It was the northern lights. They flashed on and off, lighting up first one part of the sky and then another. I thought of awakening Mama, but selfishly I wanted to keep it all to myself. Sometimes there was a falling star to wish on. I could not help but feel that like the falling star, I had dropped very far. I thought of Mr. Poe's words:

. . . the comets who were cast
From their pride and from their throne
To be drudges till the last . . .

Was I to be a drudge to the last?

The men always took Sunday off. On this

July Sunday, as on other Sundays, I looked forward to a peaceful afternoon surrounded by the thousands of logs that were our constant companions. Big Tom and Penti Ranta were fishing off the deck of the bunk shack. Papa, Teddy McGuire, and Frenchy sat near them sharpening their peaveys, poles whose sharp hooks and painted ends dug into the logs. Mama, Jimmy, and I were on the deck of the wanigan with our shoes and stockings off for coolness. Mama was mending Papa's shirt. I was brushing Bandit's fur and trying not to listen to Jimmy.

"Bet you don't know what traveling dandruff is," he said to me.

"I don't *want* to know," I said.

"It's lice. Bet you don't know what a crumb catcher is."

I put my hands over my ears, and Bandit slipped away from my lap and headed for the kitchen and the pork barrel.

"A lumberjack pickin' lice out of his clothes."

"Jimmy, that's enough," Mama said. "If you have time on your hands, you can pick the pebbles out of the dried beans."

I went after Bandit. While I was chasing him from the pork barrel to the lard bucket and back, I heard shouts. I cornered Bandit among the dried apples and, grabbing him by the scruff of his neck, put him in the cage Papa had made for him. We had rounded a bend in the river and ahead of us was an enormous pileup of logs. I could hardly believe how quickly the pileup was growing. I expected to see Paul Bunyan laughing to see what mischief he had done. The men jumped onto the wanigan from the bunk shack.

As soon as I could find enough breath to get words out, I asked, "What is it?"

"Logjam," Papa said. His voice was hard, and close to angry, as if he were mad at the logs. "The logs are damming up the river. The high water on the other side is washing logs back over the dam, pushing one log on top of the other."

Because of the dam, the logs had nowhere to go but up. The logjam was a giant monster growing and growing right in front of our eyes. Each time one log crashed against another, there was a terrible thudding sound. I reached for Mama's hand. It felt cold in mine.

The men pulled on their boots and grabbed their peavey hooks.

Teddy McGuire ordered, "Jimmy, you stay put, hear me?"

Papa said, "Augusta, you take Annabel and go inside." Mama didn't move.

The men jumped over the side and scrambled along the shore toward the jam.

"What are they going to do, Mama?"

Mama didn't say a word. She was hanging on to my hand like she'd never let go. The other hand was grasping the rail so hard her knuckles were white.

"They're going to break the jam," Jimmy said, his voice full of excitement. "I sure wish I was going with them."

The logs were crashing into one another. The jam had grown as high as a mountain. I trembled as I thought of Mr. Poe's words:

Mountains toppling evermore
Into seas without a shore . . .

The men scrambled over the logs toward the jam. They were nearly there. They looked small and helpless against the great wooden pile. Frenchy stepped onto the jam and the other men followed. I thought of how on our trip down the river we had seen a white cross on the shore to mark the graves of unfortunate lumberjacks.

In a shaky voice Mama said, "I believe I will go inside, Annabel. You'd better come, too." I stayed put. Jimmy stood next to me. For once he was quiet.

The men pushed and pulled at the logs that were jammed against the bank. One by one they worked the logs loose with their pikes and peaveys. As the logs were loosened, a little water ran through the jam, loosening other logs.

Papa made his way to the middle of the jam. He was down in the center of it.

"He's got an ax!" Jimmy said.

Papa chopped at a log. The other men stopped their work to watch him.

"What's Papa doing?"

Jimmy's voice was respectful. "Now that they got the ends free, your pa's after the key log that's holding up the jam. He'll chop it in half and the logjam'll break up. My dad told me all about logjams."

"But Papa's right in the middle of the jam," I said. I was horrified. I hated the wanigan and the river and the great mountain of logs that threatened to fall down upon Papa.

"He'll jump at the last minute," Jimmy said. "He'll be all right." But Jimmy didn't sound all that sure.

At that moment the log split. Papa jumped but wasn't quick enough. He was in the water. The logjam was breaking up every which way. It was all around him. Logs were tumbling everywhere. Big Tom jumped into the water and Frenchy followed. The logs came at them. They were swimming and dodging the logs. I closed my eyes, but I couldn't keep them closed. The men were fighting off the logs. Now Penti Ranta and Teddy McGuire were in the water, stretching out their hands to Big Tom and Frenchy, making a chain to the shore. Frenchy caught Papa by the arm. The water spilled over the breaking jam and rushed down on them. Frenchy lost Papa and got him again.

The other men dragged Frenchy and Big Tom and Papa onto the bank. Papa was safe. I ran for Mama and buried myself in her arms. I

sobbed out what had happened. We couldn't stop crying.

When the men climbed onto the wanigan, Mama threw her arms around each one of them, never caring about their wet clothes.

"I can't thank you enough," she said. "You saved my William's life."

"He's the one took the chances," Teddy McGuire said.

Papa gave a little laugh. "Never remember having so much fun in my life." He took my hand. I felt the cold and the wetness and shivered. I looked up at him. He was smiling down at me, but there was no smile in his eyes, only a look that said he was mighty glad to be there.

After they changed out of their wet clothes, the men were back in the wanigan for supper, making jokes and laughing about what had happened. I noticed, though, Mama and Papa were sitting close to one another. Later I saw the men looking out at the river of logs that floated ahead of us. They looked at them as if the logs were a raging tiger that had learned how to escape from its cage.

ALL WE SEEK TO KEEP HATH FLOWN

I awoke with a most woeful feeling. I was miserable. This was the day I would have to part with Bandit. The day before Bandit had snatched one of the fish meant for dinner and had run off with it. He was so big and strong I had trouble holding on to him. I knew in my heart that it wasn't fair to keep him in a cage, yet when I let him loose nothing in the wanigan was safe. He ate the pies Mama set out to cool. He even ate a cake of soap, so that little bubbles came out of his mouth.

"Annabel," Papa had said, "the best thing for Bandit is to let him go."

"Just think how happy he'll be to make friends with other raccoons," Mama said.

I held out for two days but today was the day. Since it was a special day, Mama let me give Bandit a pancake, which he ate in dainty bites, making scallops as he turned it in his clever paws.

With Bandit in my arms, Jimmy and I waded onto the sandy shore. The land there had not yet been timbered. Instead of acres and acres of stumps, there were tall pines. We walked under the branches of the giant pines, their fallen needles soft under our feet, their fragrance all around us. A hawk with a red tail took off from an overhead branch. Deerflies buzzed around us. A crow whose caw was half bark and half cough scolded us.

"It's too empty here," I said. It was. The shade from the feathery pine branches kept out flowers and grasses. I didn't think it would be a cheerful place for Bandit to live. We kept walking until the land dipped and we came to a bowl of timbered land. There were grasses and shrubs where little brown birds flew in and out. A narrow creek, almost hidden by the grasses, divided the bowl in half. Jimmy looked at me and I nodded.

We settled down in the grass. I scratched Bandit behind the ears the way he liked and gave him a kiss. Jimmy patted him on the head. I opened my arms and let him go. At first Bandit just sat there, but after a minute he

ambled down to the stream. He stuck his nose into the water. In a minute he was back on the grass, a wriggly crayfish in his paws. We could hear the crackle as he bit into the poor crayfish's shell.

Soon he was running off into the meadow, not even looking over his shoulder. I thought of Mr. Poe's sad line: *"All we seek to keep hath flown."* First I had lost my dog, Bandit. Now the little raccoon was gone. I couldn't help the tears.

"Maybe I shouldn't have given him to you." Jimmy gave me a quick look.

I thought about what he said. It was true. If I had never set eyes on Bandit, I wouldn't be sitting there crying.

Finally I said, "I'm glad you gave him to me. If I hadn't been so happy with Bandit, I wouldn't be so sad about losing him."

Wild canaries swayed in the tops of the yellow mullein plants. A bumblebee buried itself in a blue flower. A chorus of cicadas was humming the same tune over and over.

Jimmy's voice sounded hoarse. "My ma used to tell me stories and make me cornbread, and I sure wouldn't have gone without a ma, even though I did lose her."

I could see Jimmy was embarrassed at telling me how he felt, for he jumped up, shouting, "Bet I can get you lost."

The next minute he disappeared. I had followed him into the woods, not paying attention to where we were going. Now I had no idea which way to head.

I called Jimmy's name a couple of times, but there was no answer. I started off in one direction, but after a minute or two, I came to a tangle of blackberry bushes that seemed unfamiliar. Either I was walking in the wrong direction or I hadn't noticed the bushes before. The briers caught at my skirts and scratched my legs. The deerflies got caught in my hair. I changed direction. I began to search for the little stream. I thought I could follow it, for it must flow into the river. The little stream had disappeared. I tried another direction and found nothing but piles of slash, the branches the lumberjacks had cleared from the trunks. The slash was as high as my head and there was no way I could climb over it.

In the distance I saw pines and walked toward them. But when I reached them, I found they were not nearly so tall as the pines Jimmy and I had walked through.

Everything around me was unfamiliar. I felt as if I had entered a huge building with a thousand rooms and no way out. I thought of hungry bears and wolves.

There was a quick movement behind a bush. Not a bear or a wolf, but Jimmy. "Told you I'd get you lost."

I hated Jimmy. I wouldn't say a word to him but dragged sullenly along behind him. When we got to the wanigan, I climbed on board, still furious. All I could think about was getting even.

After supper I had my revenge. Teddy McGuire brought out his violin. He accompanied Penti Ranta in "Marching Through Georgia," a favorite of the Union soldiers. "Hurrah! Hurrah!" Penti Ranta sang. "We bring the jubilee! Hurrah! Hurrah! The flag that makes you free!" He sang with much spirit and we all joined in the chorus.

"Now, Jimmy," Teddy McGuire said, "let's hear 'The Flower of Kildare.'"

Jimmy's face turned red from his ears to his forehead.

"No, Pa," he pleaded.

Teddy McGuire gave Jimmy a stern look. "Now, boy, don't make me coax you. God gave you a fine voice. Use it."

Jimmy looked as if he might jump over the deck and flee into the woods, but his father's eye was on him. Still blushing, Jimmy stood up and began the song. The words were pretty enough, with much about beating hearts and sweet kisses. I could see how it pained Jimmy to sing such words in front of everyone. I was standing at the back of the deck behind the others. As he sang, "Soon will my heart beat with joy," I clasped my hands over my heart. As he sang, "Again her sweet kisses I hope to receive," I made kissing motions with my mouth. You wouldn't think it possible, but Jimmy got even redder. When he finished, he didn't wait for applause but stormed over the side of the wanigan and disappeared into the bunk shack. He wasn't seen again that night.

Before I went to bed that evening, I asked Mama, "Why is Jimmy so nice sometimes and so hateful other times?"

Mama smiled. "Well, dear, Jimmy is a good and kind boy, but I believe his soft heart embarrasses him. He thinks it more manly to be rough and bold, but I'm sure his good nature will always get the better of him. And, Annabel, it would be kinder if you stopped tormenting the poor boy. Don't think I missed your taunting him tonight."

"But, Mama, he—"

"Now, Annabel, that's enough. Go to sleep."

But I lay awake for a long time thinking about Bandit alone in the woods and whether I would ever speak to Jimmy again—and whether he would speak to me. At last I imagined I was queen of an enchanted forest where wolves and bears did my bidding and I had a castle full of well-behaved raccoons.

THE MOSSY BANKS

When I awoke the next morning, I hurried as I always did to look out the window. Each day I found something new to see. A great blue heron swept by, legs arrowed out behind it. A kingfisher was perched on a branch looking for small fish. A mink slunk in and out of the logs. There were high banks on either side of the river. A deer was grazing on the crest of the south bank. I resolved to tell no one about the deer. Tasty as venison was,

I didn't want to see the graceful deer on my plate.

Papa and the other men ate their breakfast quickly. There had been little rain and the river was low, leaving many logs high and dry. The men were now working the riverbanks from sunup to sundown.

I watched them climb over the deck and wade ashore. The Indian, Big Tom, stood beside me for a minute looking out at the river. With more words than I had ever heard from him before, he said, "My people traveled this river from Lake Huron to Lake Michigan. In the same way you travel up and down a road in a wagon, we traveled up and down the river in our canoes." He sighed. "It sure looks a different river now." The next minute he was over the side and joining the others.

I imagined what the river must have been like long ago, with birchbark canoes floating down it, and with no lumbermen and no logs and no wanigan. As the canoes glided silently along, the Indians must have seen bears and wolves and all the secrets of the woods that we never saw, with our noisy traveling.

After the men left, Jimmy asked me to go exploring with him. I wanted to say no, but I remembered Mama's words. Since Jimmy had forgiven me my teasing, I resolved to put aside my anger at him for losing me in the woods. Warily I agreed.

Jimmy and I climbed to the top of the steep bank and walked along the path deer had made on the bank's crest. Mr. Poe had written of such "*mossy banks and . . . meandering paths.*"

Jimmy and I had a fine view of the river and the harvest of logs that floated along on its surface. The hot July sun beat down on us. Mosquitoes hummed about our heads and needled our arms and legs.

The bank had been timbered, with nothing left but a few twisted oaks that gave no shade. Grass and wildflowers had taken root. Orange hawkweed and lacy wild carrot were everywhere. We scared up squirrels and a fat woodchuck who waddled away, stopping every now and then to look over its shoulder at us. I kept an eye out for Bandit, though I knew he was far away. Twice we found patches of raspberries and ate until the crimson juice ran down our chins.

Suddenly Jimmy stopped and put his finger to his mouth. At first I thought it was just another of his silly games, but when I listened I could hear men's voices coming from the river below us. Jimmy signaled me to stay quiet. We walked on tiptoe, keeping back from the bank so the men wouldn't see us. The voices grew louder. We crept to the bank's edge and peered down. They weren't our men. Two strangers were hunched over the end of a log. The log had been stranded along the bank when the river level had gone down.

I saw that the men had a marking hammer. "What are they doing?" I whispered.

Jimmy was watching the men. His mouth was a little open.

"Why are those men marking the logs here along the river?" I asked, still whispering.

"They're timber pirates," Jimmy whispered back. His eyes were very large. "Look at the mark they're making. They're putting a circle right around our star. They'll say that's their mark. A circle around a star. They're stealing our logs."

Sure enough. They moved on to another log with our star and hammered a circle on that one. When they finished, they wedged their pikes under the logs and sent them down the river. When the logs reached the mouth of the river in Oscoda, the timber pirates would claim them for their own.

With the logs safely in the river, the men got ready to move downstream.

"We ought to go back and tell our papas," I whispered.

Jimmy shook his head. "By the time we get back, they'll be on their way, stealing our logs farther downstream."

"We've got to stop them," I said. I was furious. It wasn't right that they should steal our logs and then get away.

"I got an idea." Jimmy looked at me. "You game?"

"Sure." Inside I wasn't so sure.

"I'm going to make them chase me. When they take off after me, you go and get their marking hammer. After you've gone a distance, throw the hammer someplace where they can't find it but remember where it is. Don't wait for me. Just run back to the wanigan and tell the others."

Before I could say a word, Jimmy stood up and began running and shouting at the same time.

The men dropped what they were doing and stared up at Jimmy. He was making so much noise crashing through the underbrush and throwing stones down at them it sounded like more than one boy. The men began climbing up the bank. I crouched down, but they were after Jimmy and never noticed me.

The minute they were out of sight, I took a deep breath and began slipping and sliding down the sandy bank, skinning my knees and bottom. I was tumbling so fast I thought I would go right into the river, but at the last minute I caught on to a pine seedling growing from the bank and broke my fall. For a moment I was too scared to move, but I thought of Jimmy being chased by those evil men and I kept going.

The marking hammer was just where they left it. Hanging on to the heavy hammer with both hands, I started back along the river toward the wanigan. My arms felt like they were being pulled out of their sockets. I didn't know how long I could carry the hammer, but I wanted to get far enough away so they couldn't guess where I had thrown it.

The banks rose almost straight up from the river, so I had only a few inches of shore to stumble along. Part of the time I was in the river, climbing over old logs and slippery boulders. All the while I was worrying about Jimmy and what the men might do if they caught him.

A small creek joined the river. There were no logs in the creek. I held tightly on to the marking hammer and swung it back and forth and then let it go. It landed in the middle of the creek with a big splash. I was sure they would never find it, but I would know where it was because there was a lone pine to mark the spot.

I scrambled back up the bank and headed for the wanigan. Though I was running as fast as I could, it seemed farther than I remembered. As I rounded each bend, I thought I would see our shack. I couldn't catch my breath. For a terrible minute I wondered if I was running in the wrong direction, but I was sure the river had been on my right.

Suddenly, below me, there was the wanigan. I shouted, "Timber pirates! They're after Jimmy! Quick!"

Papa and Big Tom and Frenchy were just below me in the river, prizing out a log. Papa climbed the bank, Frenchy right behind him. Farther down Penti Ranta and Teddy McGuire had heard me and were running toward us.

I blurted out my story and in seconds they were on their way. Papa called over his shoulder that I was to go down to the wanigan. I turned slowly in that direction, but as soon as I had caught my breath I hurried after the men.

I could hear them thrashing through the woods shouting Jimmy's name. More shouts. Jimmy's voice. Then the angry voices of the pirates. There in front of me were all of our men and—running toward them—Jimmy. Chasing Jimmy were the two timber pirates. He had managed to lead them back toward the wanigan. The minute the pirates saw how many men were after them, they spun around and began to run in the other direction. Big Tom chased them, but he was soon back. He was laughing. "They won't show their faces around here again."

Jimmy and I told our stories. On the way back I pointed to where I had thrown the marking hammer. Penti Ranta waded into the creek, held his nose, and disappeared under the water. He came up shaking off the water and sputtering. Back down he went. This time he came up with the marking hammer.

"Just the evidence we need," Papa said. "This will help us claim any logs of ours they've marked." He smiled at me and Jimmy. "I must say, you two make quite a team."

I didn't look at Jimmy and he didn't look at me.

That night a storm blew up. From the window I could see jagged flashes of lightning. A moment later the thunder boomed out. There was too much commotion to let me sleep. Mama left the lantern on for me. I lay in bed going over and over what had happened that day. Though my pillow wasn't velvet, I thought of Mr. Poe's lines:

This and more I sat divining,
with my head at ease reclining
On the cushion's velvet lining
that the lamp-light gloated o'er. . .

At last the sky was quiet and there was no sound but a gentle dance of rain on the river. I made up a story in which I soared over the forests on the back of a great eagle, flying so high that just before I fell asleep, I caught a glimpse of the whole world all at once.

THE WAVES HAVE NOW A REDDER GLOW

Mr. Poe could surely have written a poem about what happened later that night. At first I thought the shouts that awakened me were a part of some fearful nightmare. Mama was shaking me gently and telling me I must get up. I felt as if I had gone to bed only moments before, but there was a reddish glow in the window that I thought must be the sunrise.

"Don't be frightened, Annabel, but hurry and put on your things. I'll be just outside."

I got my petticoat on backward and didn't bother to lace up my boots. When I went out onto the deck, I saw that Papa had climbed over from the bunk shack. He was standing with Mama. Jimmy and the rest of the men were on the deck of the bunk shack. Their clothes were as mixed up as mine. Their suspenders were hanging, their feet bare, and their shirts unbuttoned. For the first time since I had known him, Frenchy was without his red sash.

The red glow lit up the northern bank. There was a scorching smell. For a moment I wondered if something was burning on the stove. The red glow moved toward us and above it was a black cloud. Smoke!

"Is it a forest fire?" I whispered.

Papa nodded. "It must have been set off by the lightning."

I heard the roar of a train rushing along, but there was no train, only the fire's anger. "Will we get burned?"

"No, we're probably in no danger," Papa said. "We have to hope the fire won't jump the river." I saw him give a worried look at the thousands of logs floating ahead of the wanigan.

Using their pikes, Big Tom and Frenchy began walking the wanigan down the river, away from the fire, but the fire was moving quickly.

There was a tearing noise and a fireworks of sparks as the flames leapt from the crown of one pine to the next. The fire was catching up with us. Black ash sifted over the wanigan. The smoke was so bad I could hardly breathe. Papa climbed onto the wanigan's roof. Jimmy handed him pails of water and Papa sluiced the roof. Behind us Teddy McGuire was doing the same to the bunk shack. Pail after pail was lowered, filled, and emptied.

Sparks flew about. A bit of fiery branch landed on the deck. Mama grabbed at the brooms, dipped them into the water, and handed me one. She quickly swept the branch into the river. More branches landed on the wanigan and we swept those off, too.

"William," Mama asked in a trembling voice, "ought we to get off and onto the other shore?"

"If the fire jumps the river, Augusta, we'd be safer right here in the water."

I thought of the river crowded with wood and I wasn't so sure.

Big Tom said, "This is a good river. I've

known it all my life. It's not going to give us any trouble."

But the smoke got so thick we had to wrap wet handkerchiefs around our faces.

Jimmy laughed at me. "You look like a robber about to hold up a stagecoach."

I tried to come up with something to say in return, but I couldn't think of anything but the fire. Mama was coughing, so she had to go inside. I saw that Papa wanted to go after her, but he had to keep sluicing the boat. I looked at Papa, wondering if I should go to Mama.

He shook his head. "Your mama will be all right. We need all the help we can get, Annabel."

Lighted branches, like small torches, fell around us. Papa took care of the roof. I went after the branches that landed on the deck, sweeping them into the river. When the glowing torches fell into the river, you could hear the sizzle and see a little puff of smoke. The reflection of the fire on the water made me think of Mr. Poe's lines:

The waves have now a redder glow—
The hours are breathing faint and low . . .

Three deer plunged into the river just ahead of us. They scrambled over the logs and clambered up the opposite shore. Jimmy and I looked at one another. I knew we were both thinking of Bandit and of all the birds and animals we had seen in the woods. We might be in danger but at least we were in the river and safe for now. But what would happen to the animals?

The men took turns at pushing the wanigan along. One hour went by and then another. Drops of rain began to fall. We all looked up at the sky, hoping and praying. Our prayers were answered. Sheets of rain came down, soaking the woods and the wanigan and soaking us. We didn't care. We just stood there cheering the rain.

The fire died out. There were no more flames now, only burnt trees like black skeletons and wisps of white smoke rising up from the damp earth like a crowd of ghosts.

We got no sleep that night. Mama had recovered and had tea and molasses cookies for everyone. Penti Ranta laughed and said, "If I had jumped into the river back there for my morning bath, the water would have been nice and warm."

"In Canada," Frenchy said, "we had us one *grand feu*. Dat *feu*, it lasted two days. Nothing left for miles. Next year, all green again. Wid de trees all burned up we got us good farm-land. De *feu*, it did de farmers' work."

"The lumber company that owned that land surely won't thank that fire," Mama said.

"Those trees weren't hurt by the fire," Big Tom said. "Just a little scorched on the out-side."

I couldn't help thinking of the frightened deer escaping the fire and wondering if Bandit was safe. I guess I was pretty tired because I went inside the wanigan, where no one could see me, and cried. Not even Mr. Poe, who was always miserable about something, had a poem that was as sad as I was.

THE WEARY, WAY-WORN WANDERER

It was a week after the fire when I awoke and looked out the window to see my first gull. It swooped over the wanigan and lighted onto the water. A moment later it was far overhead, no more than a white thread against blue sky.

At breakfast Papa told me, "The gull means we're nearing the end of our journey, Annabel. Oscoda and Lake Huron are only a few days' float from here."

Mama breathed a sigh of relief. I cheered

right up as well. I thought the gull was like the dove in the Bible that brought back the olive leaf to Noah because the waters had subsided from off the earth. I told myself nothing would make me happier than to live in a house perched on land. For a second I wondered if I would miss the wanigan, but the thought disappeared with the happy prospect of dry land and real houses.

Soon we saw the houses, houses and barns, and people standing along the banks of the river, staring at us and waving. I waved back.

Big Tom said, "They can hear the logs coming down the river a long time before we get here."

As we neared the mouth of the river, the men could talk of nothing but the prospect of an end to their hard, wet work. In Oscoda our logs would be chained together into great platforms called booms. The booms would be tugged to the sawmill or loaded onto boats bound for Detroit. Finally, after all these months, the men would be paid for their work.

They talked of how pleased they would be to come to the end of their labors and to receive their wages. Still, all the men seemed quieter than usual, as if they were sorry the season was ending.

Papa said, "I'll tell you, fellows, I'm through with lumbering." He gave Mama a fond look. "This year has been hard on Augusta. We'll take our wages and head down to Detroit. I've got a friend who'll put me to work on one of the barges on the Detroit River. We'll find ourselves a little house with a garden for Augusta and a proper school nearby for Annabel."

I looked at Mama and Mama looked at me. It was like the sky had opened up and you could see right up to heaven. I tried to imagine what it would be like to live in a house that never moved and to go to a proper school instead of running around the woods with Jimmy. I told myself that I would be with well-bred people with agreeable manners. Our guests would not come to dinner in their undershirts or spit tobacco juice. Instead the men would wear starched white shirts and the women pretty dresses, and the conversation would be held in polite voices. But there might be no fiddle and no songs and no dancing either.

Penti Ranta, Big Tom, and Frenchy announced that they would head back to a lumber camp in the fall.

Big Tom said he knew just where the next

camp would be. "There's a stand of pine trees reaching a hundred and fifty feet straight up in the air. You can tell when they're ready for cutting. It's the way the branches whisper to one another. It's a sound you never forget." He sighed. "Still, I hate to think of cutting them down. Soon there won't be a tree left along the Au Sable."

I thought of how Big Tom had once told me, "The river sure looks a different river now."

"After we get us a little fun in de city," Frenchy said, "our moneys dey all gone."

"Not that we don't mean to save our money," Penti Ranta said, "but every year it disappears and this year is sure to be no different." He sighed, but he didn't seem too unhappy.

"I'll be right there with you, boys," Teddy

McGuire said. "I'm heading back to the lumber camp as well." He looked at Jimmy. "My boy here will stay with his aunt in Saginaw. He'll get some education and unlearn his wild ways."

Jimmy winked at me. "You can take me to Aunt Elsie's," he told his pa, "but I'll never stay there. No hound dog ever sniffed his way back faster'n I will."

The river widened and deepened as we neared its mouth. The logs floated easily now. The men had little to do but poke one or another log to keep the wooden river flowing.

Because we were nearing the end of the journey, Mama took special pains with the meals. There were doughnuts for breakfast, and for supper she made baked beans the way the men liked them, with both molasses and maple syrup, and potatoes fried crisp with onions and lots of blackberry pie. Jimmy and I had been picking blackberries every day. There were scratches on our arms and legs and my dress had purple stains. Fast as we picked the berries, Mama turned them into pies.

For all Mama's efforts the men didn't cheer up. Teddy McGuire kept his violin wrapped up in its oilcloth. There was no dancing or songs. There were stories, but they were all about the things that had happened on our drive, the logjam and the timber pirates and the fire. The men weren't letting our trip go.

It was August when I awoke and ran to the window to see Lake Huron. Riding on the lake were schooners and steamships, tugs and paddle wheelers. There were houses and stores and a sea of logs that went on forever.

As we reached the town, Frenchy hopped over the deck and climbed onto a huge log. Balanced on the log, he floated ahead of the drive as if he were its king, his peavey raised as if it were a banner. The townspeople gathered along the shore, waving and cheering. Our journey was over and our work nearly done.

Jimmy and I watched the boom company sort out the logs marked with our star. Papa had shown the company the marking hammer, so we got the logs with a circle and a star as well. A part of our boom would go to the sawmill in Oscoda, and the rest would be loaded onto steamers and sent down Lake Huron to Detroit.

"Next year," Papa said, "you'll see new

houses in Detroit made out of boards from these very logs."

All leftover supplies from the wanigan were divided up amongst the men or sold off. The time came to pack our things. Saying goodbye was harder than I thought it would be. For the first time I realized I might never again see Penti Ranta, Frenchy, Big Tom, Teddy McGuire, and Jimmy. Ever.

When it came time to say goodbye to Jimmy, he stood first on one leg and then the other, not knowing where to look.

"We could write to one another," I said.

"Sure," Jimmy agreed. "By next year I'll probably be a chopper or a skidder like my dad. I'll tell you where we're logging."

I had put down in my best handwriting two lines of Mr. Poe's poetry to give to Jimmy:

Oh, hasten!—oh, let us not linger!
Oh, fly!—let us fly!—for we must.

They had a strange effect upon Jimmy, for he slapped his hand over his mouth. I believe he was hiding a smile, though why he should find such sad lines amusing I could not imagine.

After a moment he said, "Here's something for you." He thrust a piece of paper at me. And after shaking hands with Papa and with a very red face planting a quick kiss upon Mama's cheek, he hurried after his father.

I opened the piece of paper to find Jimmy had made a drawing of the wanigan. On the deck he had drawn the two of us standing side by side, big smiles on our faces.

Mama and Papa and I took a room in a

boardinghouse for the night. The next day we would be on a steamboat headed for Detroit. The boardinghouse was neat and tidy. Our dinner table was covered with a starched white cloth, and the food was served not on tin plates but on china plates. But with just the three of us, dinner seemed a quiet and lonely affair.

That night I slept in a real bed with clean white sheets. In the morning the first thing I did was to run to the window to see where we were. What a cruel disappointment to find we were right where we had been the day before!

Later in the day Mama, Papa, and I stood on the shore and watched as the wreckers used crowbars and claw hammers to pull apart the bunk shack and the wanigan. There was nothing left of our three months' journey. I felt as if it were me that was being torn apart.

The streets of Oscoda were sprinkled with sawdust from the lumber mill. Papa, who had once been a wheelwright, pointed to the lumber wagon's wide, flat iron tires. "The sawdust keeps the tires from sinking into the sandy roads," he explained.

Lumberjacks from all over the northern part of Michigan had taken over Oscoda. They crowded into the stores to buy new clothes and boots. Mama hurried me past the taverns, which took a lot of hurrying, for there were a great many. From a distance I saw Big Tom and Penti Ranta walking along the street. When they saw Mama and me, they waved in a friendly way, but they did not stop to talk with us. I saw that they had another life now and I was no longer a part of it.

The next morning we boarded the steamship that would take us down Lake

Huron to the Saint Clair River, Lake Saint Clair, and finally the Detroit River and the city of Detroit. We sailed past cabins and small farms whose fields ended at the lake's edge. I began to imagine what our house would look like. Papa would be working on the river barges. Perhaps we would have a little house on the water. I imagined myself watching the boats. Mama promised me I would not have to sleep amongst salt pork and flour barrels but would have a room of my own. Papa promised I would have a dog.

I thought of Mr. Poe's words:

Like those Nicean barks of yore,
That gently, o'er a perfumed sea,
The weary, way-worn wanderer bore
To his own native shore.

Of course, the river was not exactly perfumed and the wanigan hadn't been a Nicean bark, whatever that was, but we would live on our native shore. We would have our own house in Detroit. There would be shops to visit and a real school. There would be friends. I would see Papa's barge going up and down the Detroit River.

I believed my new life would be very pleasant, but I knew I would always be watching the river, hoping to see the wanigan floating by.

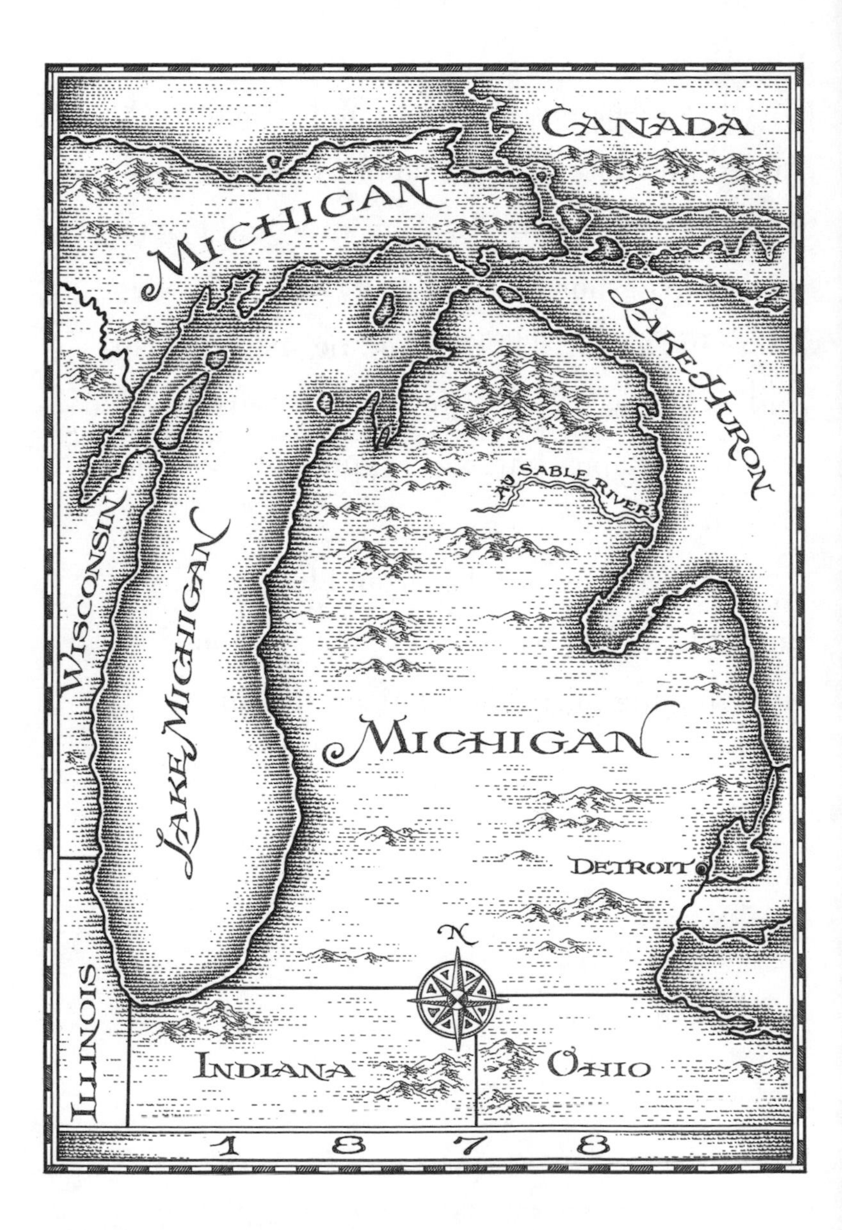
Canada
Michigan
Lake Huron
Au Sable River
Wisconsin
Lake Michigan
Michigan
Detroit
N
Illinois
Indiana
Ohio
1 8 7 8

AUTHOR'S NOTE

In the early 1800s, when settlers first came to Michigan, they thought the giant pine trees a nuisance. They wanted cleared fields for their crops. By the 1830s, pine was king in Michigan. Lumber camps were everywhere. In spring, when the ice melted, the logs were sent down Michigan's rivers, down the Tittabawassee, the Pere Marquette, the Au Sable, the Shiawassee, the Saginaw, and the Manistee. In 1850, in Manistee alone, sawmills produced seven million feet of lumber. Michigan pine was shipped all over the country. If your house is old enough, it might be made from Michigan pine. Give it a friendly pat from Annabel.

GLORIA WHELAN is the acclaimed author of dozens of books for young readers, including *Goodbye, Vietnam*, which *Booklist* called "riveting, haunting, and memorable," and *Homeless Bird*, which won the National Book Award for Young People's Literature.

Gloria Whelan lives with her husband, Joe, in the woods of Northern Michigan, not far from the Au Sable River, which she has fished since she was four years old.